Augusta Reinstein

Fact and Fancy

Augusta Reinstein

Fact and Fancy

ISBN/EAN: 9783337105846

Printed in Europe, USA, Canada, Australia, Japan

Cover: Foto ©Andreas Hilbeck / pixelio.de

More available books at **www.hansebooks.com**

FACT AND FANCY

BY

AUGUSTA REINSTEIN

PRIVATELY PRINTED

SAN FRANCISCO, 1895

THE MURDOCK PRESS

DEDICATION

———

" Come, my friend, and in the silence and the shadow wrapt apart,
I will loose the golden claspings of this sacred tome, the heart."

CONTENTS

"I love these little people, and it is not a slight
thing when they, who are so fresh from God, love us."

A BABY.

A brow so fair,
No trace of care,
An angel's kiss was printed there.

Two shell-shaped ears
With which he hears
The music of the other spheres.

O'er two blue eyes
Lids fall and rise
To give a glimpse of Paradise.

Two rose-bud lips
Through which there slips
The sweets that from life here he sips.

Ten tiny toes
Help him who goes
Over this earth of joy and woes.

A spotless soul
From which sins roll,
Perfects, completes, makes up the whole.

That is a miserable marriage, a pitiable one, indeed, where the birth of a child is necessary to reunite a couple who have become estranged.

While love must be fed by love, a love that requires such stimulation insults the passion. Yet there is something beautiful in the fact that so unconscious and irresponsible a bit of being can become a peacemaker.

Almost every day some trivial incident reveals to a lover of children a new, grand truth about child-nature. It is as true of children as of adults that they are controlled by many general rules; it is truer, that the differences in the individual characters of children must be studied to foster the best and crush the worst instincts.

The affection and aversion of children are instantaneous but just. Let all who deal with them beware that, if the former is not soon lost when won, the latter is not easily dispelled if deserved.

What an inspirer of pure thought and action is a sleeping child—and a dead one!

Emerson says, "The ornament of a house is the friends who frequent it." So are, or should be, the inmates, especially the children.

A woman who had just become a mother was asked, "Why, if there is a God, does he fill a woman's heart full to overflowing with the maternal instinct and then starve it dry?"

"You ask me, dear one, why God fills a woman's heart with the maternal instinct and then starves it dry? Who knows?"

There are many things in our experience that are incomprehensible; we must stop to reflect that we are but God's children, and are incapable of knowing what is best for us.

The child often thinks the parent cruel because he is denied the enjoyment of that which to him seems good, but which the parent in his superior wisdom knows would be detrimental to his beloved child.

There is a little bird here in my room. He is confined within the narrow limits of a cage, and sometimes, perhaps, wonders to himself why he has not a little mate to bear him company and some little ones to take care of and build a little nest for.

Suddenly he opens his little bill and sends forth a most beautiful song, as if to say, " I'll be happy anyway; I have no time to waste in sadness. Perhaps some day the good Father may send me these things that my heart so desires; but if it is not His will, I can at least be happy."

All of which is a fine bit of philosophy; still, one may say, with Bartle Massey in "Adam Bede," "It's easy finding reasons why other folks should be patient."

Why will parents persist in telling their young children how often and why they should be grateful for the creature comforts and luxuries they provide them?

The mere telling has little or no effect. It is only when we ourselves are able to make comparisons and deductions from them, that our experiences are forceful.

Still, I am not in favor of taking children to hospitals, orphan asylums, or elsewhere, to see distress of poverty, illness, or deformity, because the impression, if there is one, is transient and because childhood should be *glorious*.

I gave baby Helen a "red, red rose," but first looked to find and take off the thorns. There were none, so she was like the rose, beautiful to outward view, and with those traits which give only pleasure, not pain.

I wonder, baby Helen, will there always be some one to take the thorns from your pathway?

On the street, there came running to me, greatly to my delight (when children shun me it hurts me so), a chubby-cheeked, dimpled child, her face framed by ringlets and those by a soft swan's-down-bordered hood.

The small laughing eyes, healthily-pretty appearance, and happy activity, betokened her the offspring of a perfect marriage.

My eyes filled with tears of envy of another woman's wealth and her pleasure in possessing this child.

A few blocks farther, my homeward way was delayed and my eyes filled with bitterer tears at the sight of a baby's funeral.

I grieved at another woman's loss and the pain that must always remain, because she had once had her little one.

"It is only through motherhood that woman attains the divine perfection of womanliness. Then 'the light that never was on sea or land' shines from the windows of her soul and brightens her face with celestial beauty, like that of the Sistine Madonna."

Far, far away, up in the sky,
  God sees us every day;
But very near and just as dear,
  Our mothers watch and pray.

I have found a Madonna that I love infinitely more
than the Sistine.

Dagnan Bouveret's Madonna is a tall woman,
nunlike in face and garb. She holds her little one
close to her breast, the little face and head against
her own.

The look of utter devotion on the mother's face,
her arms, strong yet tender, twining about the tiny
form, completely express and wholly satisfy my ideal
of motherhood. Despite the halo, she is a Madonna
only in the sense that every mother is such.

The mother's dress is simple and flowing, one that
cannot fail to be artistic. The child is swathed
bambino-fashion. This, no doubt, is historically cor-
rect; but a long robe would have been more artistic.
However, in this picture as in Kray's "Lorelei,"
the upper half of the picture expresses the sentiment
of the whole.

Both mother and child are dressed in spotless

white, which relieves the dusky shadows of the dense grove.

The Sistine Madonna, especially the child, looks posed to me, while Bouveret's mother might have stopped as she walked along to caress her baby again.

The child's face is hidden here; the Christ-child in the Sistine bears resemblance to the adult Christ in the expression of the eyes.

Bouveret's Madonna is beautiful — greatly beautiful to me.

A mother should wish her children sensitive to that degree that the only punishment necessary for them for a misdeed would be the sight of the pain and sorrow caused thereby, expressed upon her face.

As deep as is my love for children is my joy that I have brought none into the world. While it lies in the power of the parents to give them much happiness, greater power is Fate's to bring them misery, agony, sorrow, and travail.

How much, if not all, of the pride of parenthood is selfish!

"This was friendship,—to laugh the lighter, to work the harder, to be gladder, to be graver."

.

E—— W——.

"There is no putting into words any feeling that has been of long growth with us. It is easy to say how we love new friends, and what we think of them, but words can never trace out all the fibres that knit us to the old."

"When I called her a little Pilgrim, I do not mean that she was a child; on the contrary, she was not even young. She was little by nature, with as little flesh and blood as was consistent with mortal life, and she was one of those who are always little for love. The tongue found diminutives for her, the heart kept her in a perpetual youth. She was so modest and so gentle that she always came last, so long as there was any one whom she could put before her."

But this little body had a soul which was not little, and a heart which was big and great.

We were schoolmates. She attracted me first, because, one day when I was ill, she came to me and consoled me by taking my thoughts from myself. "Friendship is never complete until it has been tried in the fire of sorrow. Mere companionship in pleasure is not friendship."

We read "Lucile," and with that reading began a friendship which has changed only to grow stronger.

She is small; I am large. She is frail; I am strong. She takes strength from me; I delicacy from her. I give her philosophy, the real; she sheds the glow of the poetical, the ideal, over my sterner nature.

How rich one is to have one such friend.

A—— B——.

"Friend to truth! of soul sincere,
In action faithful, and in honor clear."

A tall, straight, athletic figure, emanating great physical strength, and, consistently with it, splendid mental and moral vigor; the soul straight, strong, and sweet, like the body.

Not strongly imbued with active sentiment and poetry, yet appreciating their finest ramifications in others. Actively helpful, as well as passively sympathetic; a quick heart for charity and a vivid personality for art.

A believer in and doer of deeds, rather than thoughts, yet whose beautiful deeds are inspired by beautiful thoughts.

MY THREE GRACES.

All three are slender, spirituelle-looking women, pretending to neither beauty nor brains, but beautiful in heart and mind to all who know them well, and wise in the ways of their little world, which is, love in action.

Our friends are always beautiful to us who see the soul in the face and not the features forming it.

A hard life has not robbed them of their youth or courage or faith; it has only strengthened and sweetened them, and made them more appreciative of and grateful for the good and beauty that fall to them.

They are good daughters, good sisters, and staunch friends, with such thoughtful and generous hearts and hands, doing ever sweet if small services to those about them and those they love.

I say small services, not because they would not freely offer larger ones, but because they are beautifully consistent with their worldly wealth.

Finally, they are intense lovers of nature and art and the beautiful in every form, whether it be of thought or deed, material or of the spirit.

TRANSCRIPTION OF THE CLOSING PARA-GRAPHS OF "AN ATTIC PHILOSOPHER."

Adieu, dear friend, whom I am now to lose for a time. All that I have lately enjoyed must be laid to thee alone; for *my* friendship has been but a barren path along which I sent my sorrows, but *yours* changed it to a flowery one in returning your sympathy and practical aid.

I will think of thee often, and as often do thee reverence for those many hours of happiness thou hast permitted me to enjoy. I will repeat my thankfulness for those severities thou hast showered upon me, as they were intended for and have reverted to my benefit only.

Return again, then, in peace, and be blest, thou who hast made me vastly richer in experience and hast given me sweet memories instead of past sorrow, and accept, from the heart, my deep gratitude as but poor payment for your many good offices to Aurene.

Auf wieder sehen.

"THE GREATEST THING IN THE WORLD."

The betrothal of a young girl has much the same effect that her death would have. It lifts her into temporary prominence, and is the occasion for the discovery of many or all of her excellent qualities, latent or unnoticed before.

There is no greater sorrow than to lose our beloved dead, unless it is to lose the loved living.

There is no one both so obtuse and so acute, at the same time, as a man in love with a woman who does not return his affection.

His love makes him jealous, and therefore quick to see her real or fancied preference for another; his conceit blinds him to the truth that she cannot love him.

What a different impression is produced when a man speaks of his *affaires de cœur*, and when a woman mentions her conquests, as a womanly woman will, only " to point a moral or adorn a tale " !

When a man tells a woman that he has been disappointed in love, she thus learns that she does not hold the first place in his heart,— that she is second choice, if any. Even if their association does not tend to approach such intimacy, a sensitive woman feels hurt at such an unnecessary and indelicate disclosure.

When a woman who is still single refers to her love experiences, she allows a man to think that he stands as good a chance as the next to win her, even if he has no such desire.

There is a compliment implied in *her* confidence, the reverse in his.

The test of true love is, not that it thinks its object perfect, but that it aims to make it and itself so. True love is *not* blind.

" In the spring a young man's fancy lightly turns to thoughts of love."

The word " lightly " should not, rightly, be applied to love, unless the limitation " young man " permits its use.

Summer seems to be the time for love-making, as shown by all the summer engagements announced at the beginning of winter.

It is flattering to neither a sensitive man nor woman to be made conscious of the fact that he or she is to a high degree companionable, but not to the extent of being beloved.

> "To meet one's ideal and win, what joy!
> To meet one's ideal and lose, ——."

> "'T is better to have loved and lost
> Than never to have loved at all."

If a nature is hardened and embittered by trouble, it is better for it to escape it.

If a nature that needs it is sweetened and spiritualized by sorrow, it is best for it to pass through "cleansing fires."

MEN AND WOMEN.

How much more and more quickly women learn from their emotional experiences than men.

Men are every bit as curious as women; they are only more circumspect in concealing it. There is one trait they do not conceal so well or at all; that is their conceit.

Is this because they have so much it is bound to show itself, in manner if not in speech, or because women tempt its display?

Neither sex knows the opposite so truly as its own.

A narrow-minded woman thinks a man uncomplimentary when he praises another woman in her presence.

On the contrary, he is paying her one of the finest compliments, in implying that he thinks her so broad-minded that she can sincerely share his admiration.

It is because men, as a rule, do not understand woman's complex nature that they misjudge them; it is because women do not know men thoroughly that they think so well of them.

33

The woman who is accustomed to much attention from men should be the most grateful for every trifling courtesy; it is the woman who is not who is exacting, who does not understand that every one — and a man especially — gives only what his feelings prompt, not what would be forced.

There was a woman (forgive the libel on the sex) who loved a married man. This man (forgive the libel on the sex) excited her sympathy by confiding his marital unhappiness. She loved him for the dangers he had passed, and, although he encouraged her, after a time "He had loved her the more had she less loved him." Ever after she delighted in making men (whom she easily attracted) suffer as he had made her suffer. Exult, O *great* heart! that no such feeling, or lack of feeling, ever has entered, or can enter. If another has hurt you,— aye, even to death,— it makes you only more careful not to wound others, for you measure the depth of their pain by your own.

Life is too short, and should be too sweet, to hate or be hated.

It is precisely those men who have exhausted every vice and pleasure who seek and generally get the purest women for wives. Is this by reason of contrast, or because their worldliness gives them charms to which "the weaker vessels" readily succumb?

How can Owen Meredith, who understands woman so well, as his characterization of "Lucile" proves, say that—

"Sorrow beautifies only the heart not the face
Of a woman"?

Although sorrow robs the face and the figure of some of their freshness and firmness, it leaves a spiritual beauty that far surpasses the mere fleshly.

How beautiful a beautiful woman is,
How godlike a great man!

TWO BROTHERS.

One is tall and slender; the other shorter and stouter. One is deft-fingered and footed; the other clumsy and awkward. One is exquisitely neat in person and place; the other untidy and unsystematic.

One is fond of study, with a taste for the fine arts;

the other is indifferent to and slow in study, and quite oblivious of the higher things of life.

One is persistent in purpose; the other is easily discouraged. If the former's love were unrequited, he would annoy its object till she married him for relief; the other, if refused, would bullet his brain.

One has a quick mind, a shrewd head for business, and a faculty for saving money; the other's brain is sluggish, he has no head for business, and cannot keep a cent.

"Go forth under the open sky, and list
To Nature's teachings."

THE YOSEMITE VALLEY.

Tremendous walls of granite, — odd shapes, sometimes rising perpendicularly, sometimes domed, sometimes turreted, and sometimes sloping to a point, and always indescribably colored at dawn and at dusk.

The power and the grace of the waterfalls, the thunder of their descending, and their different ways of falling, their edges blown into tissue-veils, sending the spray great distances, the sunshine sparkles on them, turning the drops to diamonds, the rainbows arching them, the colors sometimes close, compact, and intense, sometimes spreading broad and fine.

The Merced River, — sometimes sailing serenely along, sometimes lashed into foaming rapids and cascades, rushing madly along before and after it forms the Vernal and Nevada Falls.

Great groves of gigantic trees, beautiful cloud-effects, snow-clad peaks, rich undergrowth, carpets of wild flowers, strong sunshine, bracing mountain air, and mountain water, cold and crystal clear.

THE GRATEFUL PANSY.

I nestled a brilliant pansy in the soft, dark depths of my fur cape, from which it showed its saucy face·

It faded during the day, and I found it, withered and crumpled, on the floor at night. I threw it out of the window, never expecting to see it again.

Imagine my surprise, the next morning, to find it, bright and beautiful once again, looking at me from the window-sill, where the rain had revived it to its pristine perfect beauty.

Its recovery was a reproach to me, because I knew that pansies, no matter how dead, seemingly, are readily revived.

It not only returned good for evil, but it gave me an additional day's delight.

What seemed to me to be certain death for it proved to be only renewed life.

A WINDOW GARDEN.

There are glorious morning-glories that surprise one anew every day with their delicate coloring, and deliciously sweet mignonette, dressed in subdued green, like some persons with plain faces but fine hearts.

And the tendrils of the very sweet sweet-peas, clasping their climbing-sticks as firmly as a baby's fingers hold its mother's, when standing or learning to walk.

When gathering flowers, those at a distance seem fairer than those close by; so it is with many persons, always discontented with their present possessions, always envious of what is not in their grasp.

In two gardens that adjoin is a scene that, every spring, is Chinese in its gorgeousness of coloring. The paths and circular edge of the fountain are thickly planted with hyacinths in full bloom; the long stalks are thickly studded with the starry blossoms of vivid purple and pink, light and dark-blue and pure white, outlined against the green of their slender leaves and the larger mass of green in the lawn, making one think —

"That every hyacinth the garden wears
  Dropt in her lap from some once lovely head."

If one can have a favorite flower among so many

that are so beautiful, mine is the red, red rose, the old-fashioned Jacqueminot. It has a glowing, warm color, velvety texture, sweet perfume, and perfect form. All these perfections are not combined in any other rose.

Many new varieties are being cultivated, beautiful in form and color, but often so richly developed that their heads hang down with the overweight; but my rose grows erect on its stem, meeting the sun and the dew boldly, but not too boldly, because blushingly and generously exposes all the beauty that is not hidden in its golden heart.

"Sometimes I think that never blows so red
    The Rose as where some buried Cæsar bled."

We all admit and enjoy the beauty of form and coloring and the grace of trees in summer; but to me there is a more delicate beauty in the bare branches of winter, outlined against the gray sky. They make a net of lace as fine as tracery, sharp yet soft, bleak yet beautiful.

The willow-tree especially, with its long, drooping, tapering twigs, descending like a shower of rain; then the young tender green veiling the skeleton just enough to soften the outlines, the pale gray-green vivid yet soft, strength under the delicacy, spring's balm and beauty soothing the wonderful wounds of winter.

The custom of placing marble tablets, engraved with the names of celebrated personages of all times and countries on the mammoth trees, at first seemed ridiculous and a desecration.

Ridiculous, indirectly to compare the greatness and eternality of the one with the pettiness and perishability of the other (yet the influence of a great and good man is neither petty nor perishable).

It is a desecration thus to mar the beauty and the grandeur of nature; yet, in comparing the trees, their size, height, peculiar growth, and beauty, the tablets are found to be, not only a convenience but an absolute necessity for distinguishing them.

How different robins and other small birds are from chickens, in one of their characteristics!

When a hen, or even a chick, finds a bit of bread, a worm, or other tempting morsel, she seizes it greedily and hurries to a safe place to devour it alone, but little birds, in and out of the nest, always agree, many of them joining one who has found a windfall, if not by expressed, by implied permission, his enjoyment being increased by theirs.

Do not these contrasting instincts find a parallel in human nature?

How prettily as they fly,
Are birds outlined 'gainst the sky!

Have you ever noticed how hard the little birds must strive against the strong western winds? On the avenue were some birds, busily hopping about a dull-colored mass, which inspection proved to be a bird's-nest, torn and trailing.

Even the breeze as directed by the Higher Hand could not have uprooted all this past labor. Did the despoiler consider that each soft white feather, each twig, meant a journey even if of love, of fatigue, too, for the brown builders?

Yet the homeless chirpers, undaunted at the desolation,— aye, desecration,— were cheerily trying and trusting again.

May we not learn a lesson of patience from such a scene?

Why are birds, who have known only the confinement of the cruel cage, excited to loud and continuous warbling by the sound of running water?

Is it because they imagine themselves in the tree-tops above a brook? Though they have lived in the city only, does the inherited instinct of the woodlands still live?

When passing a house that was being painted, I saw, in the garden, masses of straw, feathers, and twigs that rude, thoughtless (?), cruel, but necessary (?), hands had torn from the wood-work crevices, the cosy hidden nooks chosen by bird-instinct for safety.

My indignation and sorrow at the devastation were in proportion to my inability to remedy or prevent it.

ART.

In art, men like the feminine/figure slender; in life, they prefer the larger type. In art, the model is always tall; in life, the little woman is preferred.

Many have often wondered what action gave the peculiar pose to the Venus of Milo.

In a sonnet on the Venus of the Louvre, by Emma Lazarus, are the lines:

"Serenely poised on her world-worshiped throne
As when she guided once her dove-drawn car."

The dove is one of the emblems of love, and so is fittingly associated, and the poise of the body, with one foot advanced, might well show her driving a chariot, the floor of which was inclined, but she suggests strength so strongly that one associates a larger and more powerful animal, if any, with "Her Majesty."

There is such complete repose about the face that one prefers to have her wholly inactive.

ST. MARY'S CATHEDRAL.

One need be neither an artist nor an architect to notice some glaring defects in St. Mary's Cathedral, for they are "greatnesses thrust upon one."

No structure that is so broken in outline can be stately or grand, and we demand that impression in a church, if anywhere.

The red brick, with its sparse stone trimmings, is most unrestful to the eye. Think of it, brick for a church! Imitations of all kind are in bad taste, but brick covered with cement, to represent stone, would have been an improvement.

The building and the slated roof already have a weather-worn appearance, equaled only by our City Hall. It is not "the charm, the grace that time makes strong."

The appearance of age and decay is carried out in the back portion of the building, which looks as though it had sunk into the sand.

The lack of art is again evident in the posterior part of the structure which is so split up as to be a series of sheds.

The doors are out of all proportion to the façade of the church and to the expanse of steps leading to them. They should, at least, have been as large as the stone arch over them.

The spire is neither tall nor graceful, and the jangling chimes it promises to hold are not anticipated with rapture by the dwellers near by.

I learn that the building is in the Romanesque style, but it is no relief to know it.

The clasped hands in Amberg's " Hand in Hand" show the woman's faith in the man into whose keeping she has given her life, while her half-averted face, with its awed yet joyful expression, shows perfectly the modesty of maidenhood.

Its exquisite simplicity is simply exquisite, and recalls the lines:

" I cannot choose but think upon the time
    When our two lives grew like two buds that kiss
    At lightest thrill from the bee's swinging chime
    Because the one so near the other is."

What fine, tall, strong, heroic types in Leighton's "Wedded"! What grace in the pose, and tenderness in the sentiment!

THE TAMING OF THE SHREW.

The interest in the Daly performances is always centered in Ada Rehan and John Drew. The piece is absolutely dreary when they are out of sight.

As presented by the Daly company, the play is most boisterous. Drew, in a pompous manner, boasts of his intended subjugation of Katherine, and from the time he carries her from her home, directly after their marriage, until their return, he slashes about the stage with a horsewhip, for all the world like a slave or cattle-driver. Before seeing the play, I had thought he gained his purpose by exerting quiet strength, not by brute force.

BERNHARDT AS "CAMILLE."

"La Dame aux Camélias" is an emotional drama, and, dealing with love, and especially an unhappy love, is closer to all women than the high tragedies she enacts; and, appealing strongly, is thoroughly understood.

How many more of the finer touches of her acting one notices than in her other performances,—the hysteria, the languor of her love when its course was clouded, her childish happiness when it showed serene, the weakness of her ill-health, and her self-pity thereat, the nobility of her sacrifice, her character purified and ennobled by love, and the spiritualizing before death.

"RELIGION IS NOT A REQUISITE TO MORAL EXCELLENCE."

Why do I, who am not religious, in the ordinary sense of the word, sometimes go to church?

To enjoy the sermon as a literary treat, to feast my eyes upon the brilliant coloring in the stained-glass windows, to lose the sense of self in a large place and in a multitude of people, to experience anew the feeling of "Peace on earth, good will to men," and to have my soul uplifted, exalted, and purified by the mighty tones of the organ.

A woman adopted a little girl who had never had any "religious instruction." She asked the child to perform some service, and when the latter refused, threatened to tell God of her naughtiness. Thereupon the child screamed, and, frightened, hid herself in the folds of her foster-mother's gown.

"Think of it," said the woman, "not to know what God is!"

"Who does know?" one is tempted to inquire, until he reflects that religious discussions, like those of politics, oftener result in estranged feeling than added wisdom.

"It is a beautiful evening, calm and free,
The holy time is quiet as a nun
Breathless with adoration."

Across the way is the new Cathedral. This is a holy week, and there have been lights and music in the church every night.

Above the row of stained-glass windows is an immense rose-window; its kaleidoscopic colors are vividly outlined by its dark frame, and the whole structure, surmounted by the golden cross that gleams in the moonlight, stands in relief in the soft, pale light.

The distant sweet strains of a stroller's harmonica are drowned by the stronger, sweet tones of the organ, which swell to a grand climax as the anthem concludes and the audience passes out into the perfect night, their hearts filled so overflowingly with peace that silence is their strongest speech.

MY CREED.

I believe in the teachings of Christ, and reverence his name for his works.

I believe in the Christian principles, and try to emulate them.

I believe that love and right-doing are all that bring us happiness — love for our own and for our fellow-man as for our own.

I believe that love brings, or should bring, right-doing, or it is not worthy the name.

I believe that prayer is an appeal to the better nature within ourselves, and is not addressed to any power without and unseen.

I believe in the glory and the majesty and the beauty of the universe, but dare not say who or what made it, since none know nor ever can know.

I believe that we are one family, and that all distinctions — social, religious, or political — are frivolous, since death, if not life, levels all.

I believe in the life here, and in no speculation about the life to come, of which none can know.

I believe that heaven is here for all who merit it, and hell, too.

I believe in fate. I am a fatalist. "*Kismet.*"

"He ate and drank the precious words,
    His spirit grew robust:
He knew no more that he was poor
    Nor that his frame was dust.
He danced along the dingy days,
    And this bequest of wings
Was but a book.   What liberty
    A loosened spirit brings!"

Why is it that these cold, indifferent men are the most be-loved?
—Prosper Mérimée's Letters to an Incognita.

I have thought of a reason why seemingly cold, reserved women are attractive to some men, but which reason is perhaps as incorrect as it is original.

To minds given to keen observation, there is always a fascination about whatever is not under-stood, and a tendency to search out its meaning.

A man dislikes to think himself resistible, and flatters himself that *he* will prove the Prince Charming to the Sleeping Beauty.

The same is true, but less often so, where the sexes are reversed.

Let me ask the question, why women who torment men with jealousy, laugh contemptuously at their humble entreaties and fling their money to the winds, have twice the hold over their affections that the patient, long-suffering, domestic, frugal Gri-seldas have, whose existences are one long penance of unsuccess-ful effort to please? *"An Author's Love."*

Is it not the old, old story of the eagerness of pur-suit and the discontent of satiety, the masculine de-sire for full power, complete control,— such as a man delights in exercising over his horse, a boy over his kite?

George Kennan, the litterateur, who visited the Russian mines and prisons, to find out whether the reported cruelty inflicted upon the exiles is true, found it, if possible, blacker than it was painted. He has given the world the fruits of his experiences in his "Century" articles, and, latterly, in lectures.

I feared to have the intensely strong impression of the magazine recitals weakened by hearing the lecturer, because so many who write well cannot read their own or another's writings, but my fear was groundless.

Thrown upon a screen were pictures of common criminals and political prisoners, banished for little or no cause, by "administrative process." The faces of the former were of the usual low, depraved type; the latter had refined, strong, and distinguished faces, were of gentle birth, educated, cultured, and rich.

The detailed history of the injustice and cruelty to each, and their constant endeavor to escape it, was pitiful and harrowing to a degree, but it was encouraging to learn of the strength of the Russian character in suffering.

If this trait does not eventually right their wrongs, nothing else can.

CHARLOTTE BRONTË.

My long-time interest in Charlotte Brontë has just been satisfied by reading her "Life and Letters." So intense was my interest that I was derelict to all duty and oblivious of all other pleasure while so engaged, but her strict performance of every duty has since in- spired me to the accomplishment of my own.

What affects one most forcibly is the unflagging persistence of purpose, the strong will. in a weak body, and the unflinching faith in spite of deep and continuous sorrows.

MAIN-TRAVELED ROADS.

(HAMLIN GARLAND.)

The country atmosphere pervading these sketches makes a lover of nature ache to leave the city. The detailing is marvelous, equal in its way to Balzac (the literary Meissonier), but the life of the class of soci- ety he depicts is as great and depressing a study as Millet's "Man with the Hoe."

SUBSTANCE AND SHOW.

(THOMAS STARR KING.)

How delightfully instructive are his picturesque phrases and fine figures clothing the soul of wondrous thought beneath!

Fitting it is that, in recognition of his reverence for nature, he rests on the green earth surrounded by the daisies he stooped to lift in life.

Their pink and white heads guard him whose soul symbolized the one color, living and dead, and whose influence rendered roseate-hued the lives of his fellow-men.

THOREAU'S LETTERS.

Thoreau's letters are the letters of a dreamer, a visionary, like most, if not all, of the Concord School of Philosophy. His theories and sentiments are highly ideal, yet, like some ideals, not unattainable.

Many of his thoughts are quaint, most of them are original. His ideas of friendship and love are strongly reminiscent of Emerson. Best of all is his ceaseless exhortation for a simple natural life and for the elevation of the soul.

PASTELS IN PROSE.

"Pastels in Prose" are short sketches from the French, daintily illustrated, and prettily prefaced by Howells.

They satisfy the literary, artistic, poetical, and musical nature, since poetry is, or should be, music.

Many of the sketches bear a refrain like a song; in others, the same words are twisted about skillfully; some are merely pretty bits of description, but most of them carry a delicately veiled meaning or moral.

The imitations of the Chinese and Japanese are most quaint, and are thoroughly impregnated with the Oriental atmosphere.

SAXE HOLM'S STORIES.

Although "H. H." never formally acknowledged the authorship of these stories, they are unanimously conceded to be hers, for there is the same sweet, strong, spiritual strain in them that characterizes her poems; the same high ideals, the same intensity and refinement of thought, feeling, and sentiment.

They are further remarkable for the fact that both heroes and heroines are equally well drawn, and because her own deep womanliness is paramount throughout.

65

"TESS OF THE D'URBERVILLES."

I agree with the author, that "Tess of the D'Urbervilles" is the story of a pure woman. Hardy seems to have a penchant for having his heroines fall from grace early in life. This is noticeable in "A Group of Noble Dames " and " Life's Little Ironies." Does he wish us to imply that the women of Wessex and other small villages are frailer than their sisters elsewhere? But since such accidents but too often befall women of the civilized world, women who are neither ignorant nor innocent, women who are well-born and bred, it can surprise no one that the ignorant, innocent country lass is easily "led astray."

For a long time I could not grant Tess's purity, because she returned to the lower life after finding Love,—Love the highest, the purest, the truest. It seems impossible that she could descend after living "on the heights," but her disheartenment at being discarded by her lover when she tells him the truth (he disappointed me deeply by forsaking her), made her desperate, and an undisciplined nature is ready for anything when in such a state.

MUSIC.

67

How much more impressive the music which dies away than that which ends in loud tones, be the tones even those which terminate a majestic climax!

One often wonders how, with all the music that has been written, anything original can still be produced, just as one wonders how, with all the millions of people existing, there are still such widely differing faces and not more and closer resemblances.

The "Angel Chorus" from "Lohengrin" begins with their approach in a burst of glorious music, as though the heavens had opened and suddenly revealed the glorious sight; with their receding, the sounds soften. An occasional loud tone seems to proclaim the return of a spirit that has strayed from the band like the stragglers of a flock of birds; their gradual and final disappearance is simulated by music softening into silence.

Walter's prize song from the "Meistersingers," the "Fountain," is a constantly rolling, rippling, ever-changing melody, like a brook that never flows twice over the same spot or over two places exactly alike.

Browning and Wagner are alike in that both have written much which is marvelously beautiful, and much which seems to be discordant,— but whether this is because it is but "harmony misunderstood," is yet an open question.

•.

" Nothing is trivial in life, and everything, to the philosopher, has a meaning."

Seated at the breakfast-table, across which the sunshine streams, I am reminded, by the sudden flashes of shadow caused by birds intercepting Phœbus' beams, of the transient darknesses that cross our lives. Our impatience and rebellion would cease did we divine what compensating good, what aim for the beautifying of our spiritual nature these sorrows are intended to serve.

"There are certain secrets taught by pain which are, perhaps, worth the purchase."

After one of our visits to the German Hospital, as M—— and I sat on a bank awaiting a car, she turned to me, after a pregnant pause, and asked, "Is not all unselfishness selfishness?"

Strange to say (yet not so, for we are *friends*), the same train of thought was in my mind, and so the answer was ready,— "Though a personal happiness results from an unselfishly conceived action, that feeling is the result, not the motive, for the deed." In other words, "To be good is to be happy."

Soon after, the same idea was found better expressed in "Kathrina":

"If I make my happiness
The motive for my act, I spoil it with the taint
Of selfishness."

When passing my ideal house, whose sweet gar-
den-growths seem typical of the lovely life indoors,
I heard the snowy-haired grandmother say to her
healthily-pretty grandchild, both enjoying the early
morning sunshine: "When I was riding to town yes-
terday, I smelled something so sweet on my dress.
When I looked down I saw the violets you had given
me, and then I thought of you."

Such appreciation and praise of a child's thought-
fulness (or any one's) cannot fail to make considera-
tion for others habitual. "Let us not look down
upon the child's simple acts of generosity. It is
these which accustom the soul to self-denial and to
sympathy."

Instantly M——'s query came to mind: If praise re-
verts as a consequence of a good action, the desire for
it is not a conscious motive for the deed.

Another day I met this child crossing a clover-
field; over the lot the wind blew smoke from a pile
of burning rubbish.

She passed through the suffocating atmosphere, remarking: "It's horrible, but I don't mind it!"

Wise, brave little one, learning thus early to endure unpleasant experiences without complaining.

The earlier in life one learns to be strong,
The easier is life found as it glides along.

Are all sorrows sent for a purpose? Are not some sent through sheer hard fate?

"I boasted that I had yet to meet with any first great defeat in life,—had yet to encounter that common myth of inefficient characters,—an insurmountable barrier. I boasted that I believed in no such thing as forces in the world that are stronger than our wills, and that the imperfection of our lives resulted from the imperfection of our own planning and doing. I boasted that if ideals got shattered, men did the shattering themselves. I boasted that I would go on rearing the structure of my life to the last detail, just as I had long conceived it. *I have learned better since then.*"

A woman had two great sorrows. Then, what seemed a great joy came to her as compensation, she thought, for her suffering. It proved to be only another agony; so she must needs sink, bodily, beneath the three trials.

Perhaps, it is just as well that all the miseries come together, since a little more or less matters not, when one has touched the depths. There is a point beyond which one can suffer no more. It is there that indifference begins.

"Nothing had availed to crush him, even as nothing ever does avail to crush a man of character. But the obstacles and torments which make no impression on the mind of a strong man, often make a very sensible impression on his heart; the mind triumphs,— it is the heart that suffers; the mind strengthens and expands after every besetting plague of life, but the heart withers and wears away."

" He that wrestles with us strengthens our nerves and sharpens our skill. Our antagonist is our helper."

.

"You should forgive many things in others, but nothing in yourself."

This statement is selfish, in spite of its seeming magnanimity. By being less forgiving to ourselves, we exact a higher standard of conduct than we do from those whom we exonerate from blame readily. We allow them to rest content with what is less perfect than could be attained by our severer judgment.

"Count that day lost whose low descending sun
Sees from thy hand no worthy action done."

This is well as a daily motto, except that one is apt to remember what good has been done and to exaggerate trifling deeds to importance.

Substitute instead, "He who does a kindness should never remember it," and "Do good by stealth and blush to find it fame," even to one's self.

"Animals are such agreeable friends,—they ask no questions, they pass no criticisms."

Are not the sudden spring and bark of greeting, the scowl and growl of the dog; the purring and rubbing, the spitting, scratching, and arched back of the cat; the fiery eye of the horse, and the approach and retreat of all these otherwise unlanguaged creatures as expressive of liking and dislike as the silent actions or words of approval and disapproval of human beings?

"If by any device or knowledge
   The rosebud its sweetness could know,
It would stay a rosebud forever,
   Nor unto its fullness grow.

And if thou couldst know thy own sweeetness,
   O little one, perfect and sweet,
Thou wouldst stay a child forever,
   Completer whilst incomplete."

The incomplete man is necessarily imperfect, because undeveloped. One admires less the innocence of ignorance than the wisdom which comes through being tried by fire.

There is no strength without struggle. A negative goodness that has never been tempted or tried is not worth much.

What mother wishes her baby to be a baby always? Does she not find pleasure— her very life, in fact, now as she did before it came —in anticipating its growth, bodily, mentally, and morally, eagerly, yet fearfully?

Undoubtedly the purity of an untried soul is admirable, to a degree, as Rita finds in "Flagoletta":

"Do you know, if there is one thing irresistibly alluring in my eyes it is the freshness of an unspoilt life,—a youth with all its hopes and desires and dreams unsullied by knowledge of evil, unspoilt by contact with sin, before whom the world lies as a field to tread, not a burying-ground to shun, and yet it is the one thing we are all most anxious to lose, most heedless of possessing."

An always interesting study to a keen observer and lover of children — love of any kind stimulates observation in that direction — is the sight of youth budding into maturity. It promises so much, and one is curious to learn whether the promises are fulfilled.

The half-blown rose gives but a glimpse into its glowing heart, thus showing a delicate reserve and confining its sweet perfume. It, however, is not so beautiful as the full-blown flower, except that the latter invariably suggests that it must soon die.

" Tell them, dear, that if eyes were made for
    seeing,
Then beauty is its own excuse for being."

WHAT THE SMOKE SAID.

For some weeks I was compelled to lie abed, in perfect quiet, in a darkened room. I could not read or write or see any one but the nurse who attended me.

At first I felt so weak and weary, the absolute rest was welcome, but as I gradually grew stronger, I sought some entertainment, and found it on the window-blind.

The smoke from a chimney close by was blown by varying winds into varying shapes across it; it was not only a timepiece for me, but was also a measure of my neighbor's meals, there being more smoke at luncheon than at breakfast, and more at dinner than at luncheon.

Not long ago a little boy was gazing intently out of a schoolroom window. In reply to his teacher's question, as to what interested him so, he exclaimed, "I'm sure the lady in that house has company, for there's a fire in the grate." So the smoke from this chimney was "company" for me for many hours during those long days, and this is what it told me:

At first there came a thin, indistinct, wavering line,

like the vague, uncertain, wondering movements of a baby.   As the flakes gained in number, the air bore them along rapidly, so that they looked like a flock of flying birds, or like children racing, or like leaves dropping from the trees in autumn.

At times a strong wind sent the shadows along so swiftly they left no distinct impression on the curtain or on the retina, the curtain of the eye ; these seemed to me like the impetuous actions of youth.

The large flakes, coming regularly and rapidly, looked just like a flag fluttering in a stiff breeze, and when they came irregularly, they changed to a line of clothes flapping in the wind on a day in March.

When the smoke poured out thickly from the pipe set into the chimney, the cylinder became the smoke-stack of a steamer about to set out on a voyage, while a small, steady stream brought the steamer back into port.   Sometimes the pipe sent out swiftly, smoke and soot and cinders that made of it a cannon belching forth destruction or a man-of-war's friendly salute of welcome or farewell.

As the smoke rolled slowly out and along in volumes, it reminded me of masses of snow, the thought of which cooled my hot head—or of flocks of fleecy sheep that called to mind long stretches of flowery meadows and sunny hillsides that one longs for in the depth of winter or when a darkened hour makes winter indoors.

When there was little or no wind, the smoke passed onward slowly, like the certain steps of mature life, or with the dignity of a courtly pageant, or with the majestic movements of a camel, beneath and around him the limitless desert of gray sand, while a part lifted and curled itself above him into a stately palm.

When it was blown downward with force, it became a shower, and when denser, a downpour of rain blown to whiteness by a storm. Sometimes it descended very slowly and spread itself out into a fine tissue—a bridal veil—with dark spots here and there for the embroidery.

As the fire died down, the stream grew smaller and smaller, in the end as it was in the beginning, second childhood as weak and helpless as infancy, until it was no more, and I, too, had passed into the land of shadow, to sleep.

Have you ever seen a humming-bird poised in air by rapid winging, dipping his needle-like bill into fuchsias and other bell-shaped flowers?
Irresistible dimples,
An orchard in bloom,
A fruit-tree in blossom,
Clouds sun-tipped to silver,
The softening effects of twilight,
Shadow-pictures made by the fog,
Dazzling sunrise-sparkles on the ocean,
Brown birds on the bare branches in winter,
The long, deep curves of skimming swallows,
The alternating colors of a flock of flying pigeons,
Firelight glow on faces surrounding the hearth,
Sunlight lighting up soft hair to golden or auburn tints,
The fascination of curves not developed into coarseness,
A face spiritualized by temporary pain or chronic suffering,
Rose-petals deepening in tint toward the heart of the flower,
The iridescent burnished breast of a pigeon changing in the sunlight,
The picturesqueness of a snowstorm with the birds flying affrighted through it?

WINTER.

A dark, wet night! The shifting clouds vary from white and gray to black, and make the sky beneath pitchy. Here and there a blotch of black yawns from its white environment; it looks like our future, the deep, unfathomable beyond.

The wind through the trees sways them with a doleful strain; the reflections of the street-lamps, lying along the ground, quiver with their fitful source and vanish in a point into the darkness.

The leaves of the trees are tessellated against the lighted doorways and moisture-smoked window-panes, changing them into stained glass of an ever-varying pattern.

Everything without is restlessness, save when an occasional church-bell sounds a momentary peace over all.

We are apt to think a leaf in the calendar has been misplaced when we are surprised by a shower in summer. We bear the temporary inconvenience with little or no complaint, because we know it will not last long, that the succeeding sunshine will seem all the brighter by contrast, and that the earth and her inhabitants will be cooled and refreshed by it.

The winter rains last longer, are heavier, and wisely so, — for while the summer showers only bathe the surface, those of winter reach the seed, and quicken it into the flower and fruit of the queen season of the year.

The light summer rains are the sorrows of childhood; the winter rains, the deep sufferings of adult life, which, however, are diamonds in its depths, giving light to life.

New Year's eve, the moon was a crescent which seemed wonderfully symbolic of the time.

The small, lighted arc typifies the past, our experience during which should be some assurance of our ability to combat the future. That, in turn, is represented by the enlightened portion, outlined by the thread-line of light.

"General observations drawn from particulars are the jewels of knowledge, comprehending great store in a little room."

We are not responsible for our innate characteristics, but we are responsible for their education to good or their lack of cultivation to evil results.

In correcting a fault, we generally act its extreme opposite, until we find the happy medium.

How bravely we bear the wounds which *consciously* we inflict upon ourselves; how quickly we resent those which come from another!

Disfigured and deformed persons must feel as sensitive to rude staring as to persons turning from them in pity or repulsion. One should look at them with an expression which is neither too sympathetic nor all untouched by their ill-fated condition.

Blessed is he and his who has the faculty of finding much in little, or the broad-minded intellect and imag- -ination which sees something where nothing seem- ingly exists.

"Those who trust us educate us." How much nobler the faith which uplifts than the distrust which degrades both itself and the suspected!

It is with traveling to far-off countries as with visiting distant friends. One makes an effort to get to see those persons and places not easily reached, thinking he can always "run in" to those near by. That is why our own country and our neighbors are so often neglected.

The *Autocrat* says, "A pun is, *primâ facie*, an insult to the person you are talking with." This, of course, is an exaggeration, but it is no exaggeration to say that a voluntary apology is such. A forced apology should never occur. The tendency to excessive apology is an evidence of lack of breeding.

While we always wish to appear at our best, it is infinitely more complimentary to give others the benefit of the doubt that they do not understand the situation or condition for which we would present excuses.

While one by no means expects or even hopes to find a perfect being, it is necessary to have ideals for the maintenance of a high standard for ourselves and for those whom we idealize.

While we often thus prepare our own disappointment, we oftener, let us hope, educate those to whom we tactfully present the perfect type.

One should be exacting intentionally, not to satisfy his own selfish and perhaps undeserved desires, but to present to them an ideal he thus incites them to attain.

Very few persons possess the moral courage to receive gratefully any necessary correction, just as but few persons possess the strength of character and delicacy of feeling requisite to acquaint another with his faults, misdeeds, or peculiarities, of which he is often unconscious.

Indifference is, very often, only a passive hatred.

Our self-disparagement is often as insincere as our compliments to others.

The manner in which a person both presents and receives a gift is one of the most delicate tests of character.

Have you ever noticed the opposite effects produced by the extremes of cold and warm weather? Very cold weather has a chilling, contracting influence upon a person's spirits, making his good nature withdraw into itself, and the sufferer conscious of himself only, because of his discomfort.

Very warm weather has an expanding effect, making one sympathetic with the discomforts of another similar to his own.

The constant wonder of a person as to what opinion another holds of him, especially after first acquaintance, is a stupendous conceit. Yet is not indifference to another's criticism conceit that is greater? It is unrelieved as the first is, for the former implies a complimentary deference to and desire for another's good will.

One is as sensitive to the spirit of a book or a drama as to the atmosphere of physical and moral purity which emanates from every one, and which constitutes those supposed intangible subtle impressions which found our first judgments of individuals.

Just as in the lower animal kingdom many creatures which are deadly to men are repulsive in appearance, so many a human being whose nature is unlovable, bears unmistakable evidence of this upon the countenance, which, oftener than not, does not lie.

Many kinds of flowers are readily revived when withered; grass erects itself after being down-trodden. So human strength daily recovers after exhaustion, and is often reclaimed from a close approach to death.

It is frequently so; just as we flatter (or insult) ourselves that we have grown too strong or too indifferent to be shaken by any great joy or sorrow, Fate sends something to show us how little we know ourselves or others.

How much meaning decorations for any occasion have at the time; how dead and meaningless they appear after the event!

It is never consoling to the high nature to compare its condition with that less fortunate than itself. It is the more discouraging to compare it with its ideal.

HEALTH.

When we are weak physically, Fate seems to control *us;* but when we are strong, we feel that *we* command our condition to a greater or less extent, if not altogether.

The first duty of every individual is to be perfect physically; in other words, to be a good animal. The next duty and to others is to let them be as little conscious of his being an animal as possible.

While a nature that has become highly sensitive and sympathetic through physical suffering or other sorrow may have a sweet, softening, and soothing influence, too much of such association is depressing, since we are oftener in need of active than of passive enjoyment.

The influence of such a nature does not begin to equal the inspiring, invigorating effect of a vigorous, healthy mind and body, even if the latter is not so deeply penetrative.

There is only one degree of feeling well, but a million degrees of feeling ill.

Healthy people are pretty; strong people are graceful.

Should a perfect physique be the better able to withstand an indiscretion, or should it, by reason of its perfectness, the sooner rebel? Wherein lies its virtue unless it does both?

"Forenoon, and afternoon, and night; Forenoon,
    And afternoon, and night,—
    Forenoon, and—what?
    The empty song repeats itself. No more?
    Yea, that is life: make this forenoon sublime,
    This afternoon a psalm, this night a prayer,
    And Time is conquered, and thy crown is won."

"A" thinks that your Fate comes to you, no matter where you go, and even if you do *not* go.

"B" believes with Lucile that "we are our own fates"; that there is a great deal, if not everything, in one's own activity, in going forth to meet Fate, not waiting passively for it to come to you.

"C" agrees with "B," adding that sometimes we meet not the Fates, but the Furies.

If the mysterious one who is supposed to hold the book of life offered to show you the leaf allotted to you, would you eagerly read, or would you turn aside, content to let events take their course ?

On the beach are to be found the skeletons of crabs, the limy structure crumbling to ashes under pressure. Is the end of our life anything greater?

One should deceive himself and others, where a noble end justifies the means. One unconsciously deceives himself and consciously deceives others to make his life and theirs happier.

An active life does not always imply a useful life, for a life may be full of occupation and yet be devoid of all high purpose, just as one may talk much, yet say little of worth.

Large natures love large life, indicating a whole-souled, generous disposition like their own. The difference between a Newfoundland dog and a black-and-tan exactly illustrates this.

The one is big to burliness, warm-blooded, thick-coated, large-framed, and possesses all the instincts and desires of a healthy nature; the other is puny, timid, shivers with the least cold, and always asks to be petted and coddled. The former is self-sufficient; the latter dependent.

It is very easy to be considerate and good to others when one is himself either very happy or very un-happy—in some ways.

When one has had a stormy life and the storms have passed, he should be content simply to be at peace again, and not expect any especial happiness as compensation for his trials; yet how the starved and oppressed heart craves action through some wild joy and strong and steady sunshine !

"HE GIVETH HIS BELOVED SLEEP."

I have been at a bridal to-day. It was the marriage of a spotless soul with heaven.

The day was a perfect summer's day, just such a one as our "fair one with the golden locks" loved; even the wind had stopped in its course to do her reverence, that it might not touch her harshly, she who was so gentle to all.

As I went in at the door, the birds sang about the porch as they do in the woods, that always drew her to them in her intense love of nature.

Bright-hued flowers and ferns from her beloved Sausalito breathed sweetness and strength around her, — bright-hued flowers only, — for death was not mournful to her, who welcomed him cheerily, as a friend.

Her *lips* spoke not, — in the climax of her happiness she was speechless, silent with the weight of joy, for her too heavy but bravely borne burden had dropped from her, and her wish to pass from sleep to eternal sleep was granted just *when* she wished and *as* she wished.

But some of her last words were framed by the flowers; words of faith, courage, hope, love, pain, and joy; words which told us how to live, but also how to die.

Her death was a bridal,—her bridal would have been death.

The prayer was short, simple, true, and impressive; impressive, because true; and as she was borne "Nearer My God, to Thee," we said, in a whisper:

"Take her up tenderly,
Lift her with care;
Fashioned so slenderly,
Young and *so* fair."

OUR ELAINE.

We left her in her white home, covered with the offerings of *friends*,—and above, and below, and over all, was the heliotrope she loved so. Heliotrope for our Louise; like her, so sweet, and fading so soon.

We could not bear to put her completely from sight just yet; but as she loved life dearly, in her gratitude she is glad to go back to the dust from whence she sprung, 'wept and honored and sung.'

"To live in hearts we leave behind is not to die."

I have been at a bridal to-day.

The only true monument to the dead is, deeds to the living.

www.ingramcontent.com/pod-product-compliance
Lightning Source LLC
Chambersburg PA
CBHW020804020726
47495CB00008B/2580